# For Trixie

First Edition

1 3 5 7 9 10 8 6 4 2

Printed in Singapore

Reinforced binding

Library of Congress Cataloging-in-Publication Data on file.

ISBN 0-7868-5293-3

Visit www.hyperionbooksforchildren.com
www.mowillems.com

# TIME TO SAY "Please"!

by Mo Willems

HYPERION BOOKS FOR CHILDREN
*New York*

# PLEASE say "PLEASE"!

**and**

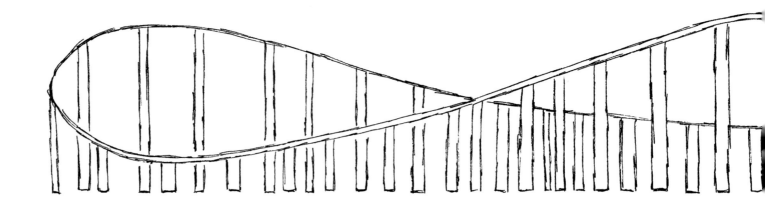

And when you want to